# THE CHERRY-PIT
# PRINCESS

*To Princess Emma,*
*with lots and lots of love.*

# CHAPTER 1

DAGNY COMFORT RACED ALONG THE SIDEWALK, jumped over the shrubs, and took a shortcut across the lawn. She reached the door just seconds before Megan Canary.

"I got here first!" she yelled.

Megan ran up beside her, puffing. "It's a tie!"

Dagny shook her head. "I was a pinch faster."

"Well, it was almost a tie," said Megan.

"Yes." Dagny nodded. "Almost."

It was hot and sticky outside. But inside, the apartment building was as cool as a giant's cave. Dagny and Megan lived on the third floor of Amber Manor, a yellow building with balconies overlooking a small park. Dagny liked to pretend she was a princess in a huge castle that had a thousand rooms. And her Mom was a queen who never ever had to go to work.

Megan pressed the UP button. "Elevator one!" she said.

"Elevator two!" said Dagny.

Dagny and Megan waited to see which elevator

1

would come first. The door of elevator one opened.

Megan grinned. "I always guess the right elevator."

"Not always," said Dagny.

"Almost always."

"Yes." Dagny nodded. "Almost."

Megan did a ballet leap into the elevator. Dagny almost leaped. She stopped herself just in time. Anna said Megan looked silly leaping and twirling. And Anna was Dagny's best friend. Anna used to live on the second floor until she moved away. This was Dagny's first summer without Anna. She tried not to think about it as she walked into the elevator without leaping.

As the door closed, Dagny suddenly shrieked, "The giant's mouth is snapping shut!"

They squealed and clung to each other until the giant's mouth opened again on the third floor.

"We're saved!" cried Dagny.

They raced along the purple hallway to Dagny's apartment, right across from Megan's.

Mrs. Comfort was counting out loud as she did her sit-ups in the living room. Her face was as red as a cherry and little curls were sticking to her shiny forehead. She took the towel from around her neck and dabbed at her upper lip.

"We got a letter today from Aunt Allie!" she said, grinning at Dagny.

"We did?!" Dagny turned to Megan. "My Aunt Allie is very nice. And she has one long braid down the middle of her back."

Aunt Allie wasn't Dagny's real aunt, but she was just like an aunt. She'd been her Mom's best friend since they were Dagny's age. When Dagny was a baby, she had spit up on Aunt Allie's best dress. Mom had told Dagny about it. But that was a long time ago.

Mrs. Comfort wrapped the towel around her neck and hunted for the letter. When she found it, she spun around, waving the envelope in the air from side to side like a flag.

Then she sat down to read the letter out loud.

*"I sure would be tickled pink if Dagny and Megan came to visit me in my new home in Cherryland. I know they would love Waxwing Orchards. I must think of something to do with Grandmother's cherries. It would break my heart to see them rot away on the trees! Maybe Dagny and Megan can come up with a solution to my cherry problem."*

"Cherry problem?" asked Dagny.

Mrs. Comfort nodded. "Aunt Allie says she doesn't have enough money to hire pickers."

"We can pick the cherries!" said Dagny.

"Aunt Allie has too many cherry trees for that!" said Mrs. Comfort. "Even if you worked all day and all night! But it *will* be good for Aunt Allie to have company. It will take her mind off her problems."

"Can we really go?" asked Dagny.

Mrs. Comfort stood up and touched her toes ten times. "I don't see why not," she said. "I think you'll have fun."

Dagny hadn't seen Aunt Allie for a long time. She had always lived so far away. But now

Aunt Allie was living in Cherryland and that wasn't nearly as far!

Megan clasped her hands together. "Oh, I hope my Mom will let me go!"

"Don't worry," said Mrs. Comfort. "I already checked. She says it's fine with her."

As Mrs. Comfort stepped into the kitchen, Dagny and Megan began to leap and twirl all around the room. Then, all of a sudden, Dagny stopped. She had forgotten for a second. She had forgotten that leaping and twirling looked silly.

"I love cherries!" said Megan.

"Well, I love cherries even more!" said Dagny.

Mrs. Comfort came back into the room with two pieces of chocolate cake topped with swirly pink icing for Dagny and Megan. "There will be plenty of cherries for both of you!" she said. "Aunt Allie has an orchard with nothing but cherries! The problem is, she doesn't know the first thing about *growing* them."

"How come?" asked Megan.

"Because she never lived on a fruit farm before," said Dagny. "That's how come she doesn't know about farms."

"That's right," said Mrs. Comfort. "Aunt Allie's always lived in big cities. It was her grandmother who owned Waxwing Orchards. And she took wonderful care of it too! When she died, she left the house and orchard to Aunt Allie."

Dagny was bobbing up and down. "So, when can we go?" she asked.

4

"I'll give Aunt Allie a call and see if I can find out," said Mrs. Comfort, as she headed out of the room again. "But I'm not sure if her phone's hooked up yet. She just moved in last week!"

Dagny and Megan soon had their mouths full of chocolate cake.

"Mmmm," said Megan. "I love swirly pink icing."

"Pink like cherry blossoms," said Dagny. "I can make up a story about cherries, if you want."

Megan shrugged. "Okay."

"Once upon a very long time ago," said Dagny, "there was a boy who broke a tooth on a cherry pit, and you know what?"

"What?"

"He got really mad," said Dagny, "and he put a spell on the cherry tree and turned the tree into a princess! A princess with a cherry-pit heart!"

"A cherry-pit heart?" said Megan. "I never heard of that!"

"Of course not," said Dagny. "I just made it up. So anyway, the King and Queen adopted her. But she wasn't nice. She was always yelling because she had a hard heart.

So then the King said he'd give gold coins to any-body who could make the Princess be nice. And you know what happened then?"

Megan just shrugged because her mouth was full of chocolate cake again.

"Well, a very brave girl wanted the gold coins so her mother wouldn't have to work anymore," said Dagny. "So she spied on the Princess."

"That's rude," said Megan.

"What's rude?"

"Spying."

"It's rude to interrupt too, you know! Now just listen!" said Dagny. "Every day, the brave girl spied on the Princess in the orchard. And the Princess kept putting her arms in the air and swaying back and forth like a tree. That's how the brave girl figured out the Princess was really a cherry tree. So she told the King and Queen to make sure the Princess kept her feet wet all the time."

Megan shook her head. "Wet feet can give you a very bad cold."

Dagny stuck her finger in the swirly pink icing, then waved it at Megan. "If you say one more word, you'll get icing on your nose!"

Megan covered her face.

"They didn't *have* bad colds back then!" said Dagny. "When her feet were wet all the time, roots started growing from her toes. Then she turned back into a cherry tree. And she liked herself better that way. Everybody else liked her better that way too. The end."

Just then Mrs. Comfort stuck her head into the room. "Aunt Allie wants you to come lickety-split!" she said. "How does tomorrow sound?"

"Yippee!"

Dagny and Megan squealed and gave the thumbs-up sign.

"I'm glad we're best friends," said Megan.

Dagny didn't say anything.

"I'm your best friend, right?" said Megan.

"Well....." Dagny thought about Anna. She thought about their promise to be best friends forever and ever, just like Mom and Aunt Allie. "You're my *almost* best friend."

"*Almost?*"

"Anna Earl is my best friend, even if she did move far away and I might never see her again," said Dagny.

Megan shrugged. "Well, I'm *almost* your best friend."

"Yes." Dagny nodded. "Almost."

# CHAPTER 2

THE NEXT DAY WAS SUNNY AND HOT!

Stinking hot! Dagny poked her head into the kitchen. Her Mom was reading the paper and drinking coffee with her elbow on the table. And her Mom always said it was rude to put your elbows on the table!

"Mom, can you braid my hair for me?"

"Sure!" said Mrs. Comfort, and she took her elbow off the table. "Braids are just what you need!"

Dagny perched on the stool. "One long braid down the middle of my back, please."

Mrs. Comfort brushed away the tangles, then braided the thick brown hair, tying it with an elastic band.

"Now go pack your clothes," said Mrs. Comfort. "lickety-split!"

Dagny hopped on one foot to her bedroom. She liked the way the braid felt as it thump-thump-thumped against her back. She hopped over to the closet and dragged out the green suitcase, the one with the zipper that sometimes got stuck. But it didn't get stuck this time. It made a zip-zip-zippy sound.

Dagny scooped up armfuls of shorts and tops and socks and underwear and dropped them into the suitcase. Then she used her best karate chops to crush them down.

"Hi-ya! Hi-ya!"

She tossed in a pad of paper, a chewed-up pencil and a letter from Anna. Maybe she would write to Anna. Maybe Anna would write back. Maybe Anna would wish she were at the orchard too!

Anna had a pet snake.

Anna could kick a soccer ball better than anybody. Whoosh!

Megan wasn't like Anna. Megan took art lessons. She did ballet leaps on the front lawn. She wore ribbons in her hair.

Dagny didn't pack any ribbons.

She gave her goldfish, Mrs. Waterhouse, a pinch of food.

"I'll be back to take care of you, Mrs. Waterhouse," she said. "I'm not moving away or anything."

She looked deep into one of Mrs. Waterhouse's popping-wide eyes. Mrs. Waterhouse looked lonely.

"Don't worry. I'll buy a best-friend fish for you when I get back. And Mom will feed you while I'm gone."

But all of a sudden, Dagny wasn't so sure. What if her Mom forgot? Once her Mom had forgotten to put the ice-cream in the freezer and they'd had to eat carrot sticks for dessert! And sometimes her Mom forgot a whole bunch of numbers when she was doing her sit-ups. Sometimes she went from ten to twenty without counting any numbers in between!

Just to be on the safe side, Dagny cut fish shapes out of paper and taped them to the bathroom mirror as a reminder. Then she zipped up her suitcase and dragged it out to the kitchen.

Mrs. Comfort was putting cookies into a bag. "For the trip," she said.

Sugar-free cookies. Yuck! Dagny peeked in the fridge, but the cake with the swirly pink icing was all gone.

"Did you pack your toothbrush?" asked Mrs. Comfort.

"Oops!"

Dagny was back in a flash with her toothbrush.

"We'd better get going," said Mrs. Comfort. "I want to check the oil before we're off."

Mrs. Comfort knocked on the door across the hall and told Mrs. Canary they'd be waiting downstairs for Megan.

As they stepped into the elevator, Dagny glanced over at the box her Mom was carrying.

"What's in there?"

"Books for Aunt Allie," said Mrs. Comfort. "I've read them."

Dagny wished she had something for Aunt Allie too. She thought about the yucky, sugar-free cookies. Maybe she'd give them to Aunt Allie. But what if Aunt Allie didn't like sugar-free cookies? Maybe she would think it wasn't a real present. Maybe she would think Dagny was just trying to get rid of them because they tasted like dirt and sawdust. But she would give Aunt Allie sugar cookies too, if she had any!

As they headed across the parking lot, Dagny dug into her pocket and pulled out two sticks of gum. She could give Aunt Allie gum too. The gum would take away the yucky taste of the cookies.

"Going somewhere?"

Mrs. Brock was shouting down to them from her balcony.

Dagny nodded and shouted back, "To Cherryland!"

Cherryland was a fun word. It had a magic kind of sound like Fantasyland and Toyland. Dagny kept saying it to herself.

"Cherryland, Cherryland, Cherryland."

She didn't stop until they got to the car.

It was an old blue car. The fender was dented. Mrs. Comfort called it "good old Bessie." Sometimes it made funny sounds. Then she called it a "bucket of bolts."

Dagny leaned against the dented fender and watched for Megan while her Mom fiddled around under the hood.

Maybe Megan had slept in. Maybe she'd changed her mind and wasn't going with them to Cherryland. Dagny wouldn't have anyone to play with. Not Anna. Not Megan. Not one person in the whole world!

The back door of the apartment building opened. It was Megan! She was carrying a yellow suitcase. She was wearing yellow shorts and a blouse with a yellow collar. And there was a yellow ribbon in her hair!

Everything matched. Even her curly hair was yellow!

Dagny didn't match. Dagny never matched. But she *did* have one long braid down the middle of her back, and she grinned as she let it swing from side to side.

"I've got popcorn!" shouted Megan.

Dagny's grin widened. Popcorn was a whole lot better than sugar-free cookies!

Mrs. Comfort threw the suitcases into the trunk while Dagny and Megan slid into the back seat and buckled up.

"Ready for takeoff?" asked Mrs. Comfort.

"Ready!" shouted Dagny and Megan.

Dagny rolled down the window so she could feel the wind whipping against her face.

And her hair didn't get a pinch messy with one long braid! She felt like the Princess of the Windstorm!

On the long drive, Dagny and Megan ate popcorn and told jokes. And Dagny talked about Aunt Allie.

"She's an artist. And she smiles a lot!"

"And she has pizzazz!" said Mrs. Comfort.

"What's pizzazz?" asked Megan.

"That just means she's full of life," said Mrs. Comfort. "And very special, like the two of you."

"I can make up a story, if you want," said Dagny. "About the Princess Pizzazz."

"I want to help this time," said Megan.

Dagny thought about this for a minute, then she nodded. "Okay. But I get to start," she said. "Once upon a very long time ago, there was a princess called the Princess Pizzazz."

"My turn," said Megan. "And they called her that because she could dance with pizzazz! She was the best dancer in the whole world! And she said she'd only marry a prince who could dance with pizzazz too!"

Dagny tapped her hand over Megan's mouth when her turn was up. "So there was going to be a contest to see who could dance the best. And every prince was practicing very hard. But there was one prince who couldn't dance at all. Not even a pinch. But he wanted to marry the Princess, so he kept trying."

"Well...." said Megan, "the Prince Unpizzazz went for a walk one day and got lost and nobody ever saw him again."

"Ha!" said Dagny. "Everybody thought he was lost. But he was really sitting in a cave trying to think up a way to marry the Princess."

"Ha yourself!" said Megan. "On the day of the contest, he stepped all over the feet of the Princess Pizzazz!"

Dagny grinned. "Oh, yeah? Well, he won anyway!"

"He did not!" cried Megan. "He didn't dance with pizzazz!"

"Yes, he did!" said Dagny. "He danced with the Princess Pizzazz, so he danced with Pizzazz! Ha, ha, ha!"

Megan crossed her arms. "That's cheating!"

But Dagny wasn't listening. She was looking out the car window at the zillions of trees all tickled pink with cherries! Sometimes the cherry trees were cuddled up next to the houses. Sometimes they stretched out far across the fields in neat little rows. And sometimes they just grew wherever they fancied — here, there and everywhere!

Dagny's foot went thump against the front seat whenever she saw a roadside stand with boxes of cherries lined up on top.

*Thump, thump. Thump, thump, thump.*

"Are we there yet?" she asked when the dusty road kept wiggling its way on and on through Cherryland.

"No," said Mrs. Comfort. "Stop thumping."

"Are we *almost* there?"

"Yes." Mrs. Comfort nodded. "Almost."

# CHAPTER 3

IT WASN'T LONG BEFORE MRS. COMFORT POINTED TO a pink house up ahead. It was sitting far back from the road, all snug and cozy in the middle of rows and rows of cherry trees.

"There it is!" she said.

"Yahoo!"

Dagny and Megan let out a yell that made Mrs. Comfort jump. "Look!" cried Dagny. "Somebody painted cherries all over the fence!"

"Oh, yeah," said Megan. "And all over the mail-box too!"

As the car turned onto the gravel driveway, Mrs. Comfort suddenly stomped on the brakes. Stretched out in the middle of the driveway was a black cat with white paws. Mrs. Comfort honked and honked the horn. The cat looked at them and yawned. But he didn't move.

"Go on, you silly thing!" shouted Mrs. Comfort. "Get out of the way! lickety-split!"

Megan leaned towards Dagny and whispered,

"What does lickety-split mean?"

Dagny whispered back, "It means fast as fast can be."

"Oh."

"Maybe he can't hear very well," said Dagny.

"Just like my Grandpa." Megan poked her head out the window, cupped her hands around her mouth and hollered, "Hey, cat! Scoot!"

The cat blinked but he still didn't move.

"Wait!" said Dagny. She reached into the front seat and grabbed the bag of cookies.

Mrs. Comfort glanced into the mirror. "What are you doing with those?"

"Just watch!"

Dagny took a cookie from the bag and threw it out the window. It landed in the tall weeds at the side of the driveway. The cat's ears perked up and he got to his feet. He moved slowly towards the cookie.

"Thank goodness!" said Mrs. Comfort.

As the car started moving again, Dagny twisted around to look out the back window.

The cat sniffed at the yucky cookie, then walked away.

Up ahead, Aunt Allie was waving to them from the front porch, with her arms high in the air.

The car slowed to a stop and they piled out. The air was thick with the sound of insects and everything smelled of flowers and dried grass.

Aunt Allie came running across a lawn splashed with dandelions.

"Hallooo!"

She threw her arms around Mrs. Comfort and

Dagny. "I'm tickled pink you came!"

And then she hugged Megan. "Please think of me as your Aunt Allie too, okay?"

Megan grinned. "Are all those trees yours?"

Aunt Allie laughed. "Every one of them."

"How many do you have?" asked Dagny.

"Three hundred," said Aunt Allie. "But I don't know what I'm going to do with all those cherries. I don't have enough money to hire pickers. And that means the cherries will go to waste, and I might even have to sell Waxwing."

*"Sell?!!"*

Dagny and Megan and Mrs. Comfort all cried out at once.

Aunt Allie sighed a big sigh. "I don't want to. I love it here. But if I can't hire pickers, then I can't sell the cherries. And without the money from the cherries, I just can't afford to pay the taxes."

"We'll think up something," said Dagny.

"I'm afraid it would take a miracle," said Aunt Allie. "But let's not worry about that right now. Why don't you and Megan take a look around while your Mom and I have a nice cup of tea?"

They didn't wait to be asked twice. It felt good to run after sitting for so long. They played tag and hide-and-seek and ran all over the orchard. They played until their elbows were dirty, their knees were stained green from the grass, and their hair was tangled.

Then they climbed into some old crates hidden in the long grass and pretended they were sailing on a stormy sea, using sticks for oars and rowing very hard.

When Dagny got tired of playing lost-at-sea, she kicked over her crate and stood on top of it.

"What are you doing?" asked Megan.

"Standing on a stage," said Dagny.

Megan stood on her own stage.

They took turns singing cherry songs.

They sang very loud. Nobody told them to be quiet. Nobody told them they were bothering the neighbours. They pretended the cherry trees were people. They sang and the tree-people clapped.

"Listen to this one," said Megan. She took a deep bow. "*Cherry trees are wonderful, they don't get lost at sea, and when I get real thirsty, I make cherry-berry tea!*"

"My turn!" said Dagny, and she cleared her throat. "*I put cherries in my pockets, I put cherries in my rockets, I put cherries in my locket, cause I love, love, love cherries!*"

"Hmmm," said Megan.

"Hmmm, yourself!" said Dagny, putting her hands on her hips.

Megan made a face. "A locket is something you wear around your neck."

"So?"

"So it's tiny. You can't put cherries in a locket!"

"I meant a *picture* of cherries," said Dagny.

"People don't wear pictures of cherries around their necks," said Megan.

"You don't know what people wear!" yelled Dagny. "You don't know everything, Megan Canary!"

"You don't have to get mad," said Megan.

Dagny grinned. "Let's do a song together. I'll

sing some, then you sing some."

They stood side by side and bowed.

Megan boomed out, "*An orchard is a nice, nice thing!*"

Dagny gave a little kick with her leg. "*It's where I like to go and sing!*"

"*Or sometimes I just like to hum!*" sang Megan, giving a little kick too.

Then Dagny finished by kneeling on one knee and stretching her arms out wide. "*Come to my orchard! Please, please come!*"

Megan began to leap and twirl all around the crates. Dagny wished it wasn't silly to leap and twirl. She'd leap and twirl too if it wasn't silly.

Suddenly Megan lost her balance and grabbed onto Dagny. They both tumbled into the long grass, rolling around and laughing. They laughed until they couldn't laugh any more. Not even a pinch. Then Megan stretched out flat, her eyes closed and her mouth opened wide.

"Are you dead?" asked Dagny.

Megan nodded.

"Dead as a doornail?" asked Dagny.

Megan nodded again.

Dagny pulled out a handful of grass. "I'll save you with magic pizzazz!" And she sprinkled grass all over Megan's face.

"Stop it!" Megan cried, sputtering out bits of grass. "Grass has spider spit on it, you know!"

"Spiders can't even spit!" said Dagny.

"Can so! How do you think they make their webs?"

Dagny shook her head. "I read about spiders. They

do *not* spit. They've got special spinner things that make the webs."

"Ha!"

"Ha yourself!"

Megan got to her feet and started heading back to the house. Dagny ran to catch up to her.

"We've gotta think up something, right Megan?" she said. "So Aunt Allie won't have to sell the farm, I mean."

"Waxwing isn't a farm," said Megan, as she brushed the grass from her blouse with the yellow collar. "It's an orchard."

"It's not *just* an orchard! There's a house and a shed and stuff."

Megan thought for a moment. "Are there any animals?"

"Just the cat," said Dagny.

Megan shook her head. "There's supposed to be a cow or a pig for it to be a farm."

"Well, it's *almost* a farm."

"Yes." Megan nodded. "Almost."

# CHAPTER 4

DAGNY AND MEGAN FOUND MRS. COMFORT AND Aunt Allie in the kitchen drinking tea.

"How in the world did you get dirty so fast?" asked Mrs. Comfort.

Dagny glanced down at her grass-stained knees. "We're just a pinch dirty."

"Staying clean isn't any fun!" said Aunt Allie.

Mrs. Comfort rolled her eyes to the ceiling. "Well, just be sure to have a bath before bed."

"I'm going to have a bubble bath," said Megan, "with lots of bubbles to wash away all the spider spit."

"There's no such *thing* as spider spit!" cried Dagny.

"Ha!"

"Ha yourself!"

"Keep that up," said Mrs. Comfort, "and Aunt Allie will be sending you home with me, lickety-split!"

Aunt Allie laughed. "Not a chance."

Mrs. Comfort finished the last drop of tea and they

walked her out to the car.

"I'll miss you," she said, giving Dagny a big hug.

Dagny felt a lump in her throat. She'd miss her Mom too. No one else knew how to tuck her in at night with the blankets all snug. She sniffed as her Mom started up the car.

Mrs. Comfort gave a couple of toots of the horn, then she was gone.

Dagny rubbed a hand across her eye, hoping nobody had seen the tear that trickled down. Then she followed Aunt Allie and Megan across the dandelion lawn and back into the house.

Aunt Allie made them pink lemonade and showed them her paintings of cities. Cities all lit up at night. Cities piled high with snow. Cities splish-splashy in the rain. Cities on a hot summer's day.

"You sure like cities!" said Megan.

Aunt Allie smiled. "Cities are what I know."

"I think these are really good!" said Dagny.

"Thanks," said Aunt Allie. "My favourite thing in the world is a blank canvas. It's just waiting for someone to give it a splattering of pizzazz!"

Megan was holding up a canvas. "Who's this?" she asked.

It was a girl with thick brown hair like Dagny's. It looked like a kid had painted it.

"That's my best friend!" said Aunt Allie.

Dagny's eyes widened as she looked over at the painting. "Is that my Mom?"

"Yes, sirree!" said Aunt Allie. "We were about your age when I painted that picture. We had just decided to be best friends forever and ever!"

"She looks happy," said Megan, and her voice had a wiggle in it like the road through Cherryland. "I'd look happy too if I had a best friend."

Dagny didn't want to talk about best friends anymore. Instead, she asked Aunt Allie about the fence outside. "Did you paint all those cherries on it?"

Aunt Allie grinned. "I thought it needed a splattering of pizzazz."

"Did the mailbox need splattering too?" asked Megan.

"I'm afraid so." Aunt Allie laughed. "And I *almost* splattered the porch!"

"How come you didn't?" asked Dagny.

"I wish I could say I came to my senses," said Aunt Allie. "But the truth is, I ran out of red paint!"

"Guess what?" said Megan. "I take art lessons."

"Really?" said Aunt Allie. "That's great!"

Megan and Aunt Allie started talking about brush strokes. Dagny opened her mouth and tried to think of something to say, but then she closed it again. She didn't know anything about brush strokes. The only thing she knew how to do was make up stories.

And she didn't think that was a bit special. Not like taking art lessons.

She cleared her throat and said, "I take piano lessons."

Aunt Allie and Megan turned to look at her.

"You're so lucky!" said Aunt Allie. "I've always wanted to play the piano."

Dagny hardly ever fibbed, but now she couldn't stop.

"My teacher says I'm very good. Very, *very*, good!"

23

"You're making that up!" said Megan.

"I am not!"

"Maybe you could teach me," said Aunt Allie.

Dagny stared down at the broken strap on her sandal. "Too bad you don't have a piano," she said.

"But I do!" said Aunt Allie. "There's one in the front room. It belonged to my grandmother."

Dagny swallowed hard.

Aunt Allie held out her hand. "Come and play something for us, Dagny!"

Dagny's sandals went flip-flip, flip-flip-flop on the shiny floorboards as she followed Aunt Allie along the skinny hallway. Her stomach went flip-flop too when she saw the upright piano in the front room, with pictures in fancy frames on top. All the people in the pictures were staring at her, waiting for her to sit down and play.

Dagny slowly crossed the room, took a few spins on the shiny stool and wiggled her fingers in the air. "I'm just getting my muscles loose," she said, looking up at Aunt Allie. "My Mom says you should stretch your muscles before you do stuff."

Aunt Allie nodded. "Good idea."

Dagny stood up and touched her toes ten times. Then she ran on the spot, lifting her legs very high.

"People don't do that to play the piano," said Megan.

"They do so!" said Dagny. "Anyway, I'm done now."

She sat down. Maybe it would sound nice. Maybe it would sound all tinkly and soft. Her fingers went all the way from one end of the piano to the other.

Up and down, up and down on the keys. But it did-n't sound nice. It didn't sound all tinkly and soft. It sounded like furniture falling down the stairs!

Megan covered her ears. "Stop!"

Dagny stopped. "I think there's something wrong with the piano," she said.

"Yes," said Aunt Allie. "It needs tuning."

"I'd play with double-dip pizzazz if the piano was tuned," said Dagny.

Just then the phone rang and Aunt Allie hurried out of the room to answer it.

"That hurt my ears!" said Megan. "I bet you don't even take piano lessons!"

"You don't know what I take, Megan Canary!"

Dagny slid off the stool and walked over to the window. She watched the cherry trees swaying in the breeze like the Cherry-Pit Princess. When Aunt Allie came back, Dagny asked if they could pick some cherries.

"Of course!" said Aunt Allie.

So they set to work filling buckets with the bright red cherries. Whenever they found two cherries on the same stem, they put them over their ears to dan-gle like earrings. And sometimes they popped them into their mouths, but the cherries weren't very juicy.

Just as the buckets were almost full, one of the neighbours stopped by.

"Oh, hello Janet!" said Aunt Allie.

She introduced Mrs. Armstrong to Dagny and Megan.

"Nice to meet you," said Mrs. Armstrong. She

glanced down at the buckets of red cherries. "You picked the cherries too soon. Those are Bing cherries. You're supposed to pick them when they turn black."

"Oh, dear," said Aunt Allie. "I didn't know that."

"All your cherries are Bing cherries," said Mrs. Armstrong, "except for a few cherry trees in your front yard, and those cherries have already turned black so you can pick them. But the Bings won't be ripe for another week or so."

Aunt Allie sighed. "I have a lot to learn."

"All different kinds of cherries grow in Cherryland," said Mrs. Armstrong. "Some get ripe sooner than others."

"Oh."

Mrs. Armstrong was carrying a pink and white case. "I have samples of the Sweetheart Beauty Products," she said. "Would you like to see them? I go door-to-door taking orders."

"Do I pay for it now?" asked Aunt Allie.

Mrs. Armstrong nodded. "That's right. And then I make the delivery in a few weeks."

"Sure, I'll take a look," said Aunt Allie. "But I'm a bit short on cash at the moment. I won't be able to buy much."

When Aunt Allie and Mrs. Armstrong went into the house, Dagny and Megan ran to pick some of the black cherries from the front yard, then they washed them under the hose. Dagny lay with her stomach across the cracked seat of an old swing. Megan perched on a tree stump. They took turns spitting out cherry pits as hard as they could.

"These black cherries are nice and juicy," said Megan.

Dagny nodded. "The Bing cherries will all go to waste because there's no money for pickers." She wished the Princess of the Windstorm would come along and blow all the cherries off the trees for Aunt Allie.

"I wonder why they're called Bing cherries?" asked Megan.

Dagny thought for a moment. "Maybe they go bing-bing-bing when they fall on the ground."

"The cherry pits go bing-bing-bing," said Megan.

"Know what?" said Dagny. "When cherries turn black, they taste like the night."

Megan shook her head. "The night doesn't have a taste."

"Yes, it does," said Dagny. "It has a black cherry taste."

"Does not."

"Does too."

"You just made that up," said Megan.

"Maybe I did, maybe I didn't." Dagny twisted the swing around and around. The rope creaked.

Megan spit out a pit. It landed on the top of a daisy. The black cat with the white paws came by. Megan reached out to pet him, but he jerked away from her and hissed. He wanted to be left alone.

"That's a dumb cat," said Dagny.

They ate cherries and spit pits until Dagny suddenly cried out, "I've got it!"

"Got what?"

"I've got the answer!" cried Dagny. "The answer to the cherry problem, I mean."

27

Megan tucked a buttercup behind her ear. "So what's the answer?"

"We can go door to door, like Mrs. Armstrong!" said Dagny. "We can get a zillion orders for cherries! The neighbours can pay us now, then Aunt Allie will have enough money for pickers!"

"I was just thinking of that," said Megan.

"Of what?"

"Getting a zillion orders for Aunt Allie."

"You were not!" cried Dagny. She kicked off her sandals and spun around as the rope untwisted. "It was *my* idea! And it's *my* Aunt Allie!"

"She's not your real aunt," said Megan.

"Well, she's *almost* my aunt!"

"Yes." Megan nodded. "Almost."

# CHAPTER 5

DAGNY AND MEGAN GOT UP EARLY THE NEXT morning so they could get started going door-to-door.

Dagny put on the blue shorts her Mom had made in sewing class, her 'first try' shorts. The pocket was crooked and sewn shut. Megan was wearing white shorts with pink pockets shaped like hearts. Dagny wished she had pockets shaped like hearts.

When she tried to make one long braid down the middle of her back, it turned out crooked like her pocket, and bits of hair were sticking out all over the place. But Megan said it was *almost* down the middle of her back, just a pinch crooked and messy.

Aunt Allie made pancakes and bacon for breakfast. And there was lots of chocolate milk. They dried the dishes, then set off down the road lickety-split with a notepad and pencil, turning in at the first driveway.

Mrs. Armstrong was in the backyard hanging laundry on the line. "Hi there!" she said. "How nice to see you again."

Dagny looked at all the white sheets and towels. They reminded her of Aunt Allie's blank canvasses.

"Your laundry is waiting for a splattering of pizzazz," she said.

"A splattering of what?!"

"Pizzazz," said Dagny.

"Oh, I don't want them splattered," said Mrs. Armstrong. "I like them white."

"How come you don't use a drier?" asked Megan.

"I like the way the clothes smell when they dry in the sun," said Mrs. Armstrong. "All nice and fresh."

"We don't have a clothesline," said Dagny. "There's not enough room on our balcony."

Mrs. Armstrong smiled as she bent to pick up a wooden clothespeg from the long grass and held it between her teeth.

"Would you like to order some cherries?" asked Dagny. "Black cherries."

"I shav shish sherry shees."

"Pardon?"

Mrs. Armstrong took the clothespeg out of her mouth. "I have six cherry trees."

"Oh," said Dagny. "Thanks anyway."

They walked a bit farther until they came to a leaf-green house. A white-haired man was standing out front, painting a roadside stand bright red. He was whistling while he worked.

"Excuse me," said Megan. "Would you like to order some cherries?"

"Cherries?" The man put down his paint brush and leaned on his cane. "Oh, dear, no. We planted a cherry tree every time one of our grandchildren was

30

born. We've got fifteen cherry trees."

"Too bad," said Megan.

They stood for a moment watching the man's cheeks puff out as he whistled.

"Are you whistling to the birds?" asked Dagny.

"Oh, dear, no," said the man. "I'm composing a poem. I think better when I'm whistling."

"I can make up a poem," said Dagny.

The man said he'd like to hear it, so she took a deep breath and began:

> *"I can eat a zillion cherries,*
> *I can eat them lickety-split,*
> *But even if I'm hungry,*
> *I'd never eat a pit!"*

"Aaaah!" said the man. "It's nice to meet a fellow poet. My name is Mr. Harcourt."

Dagny shook his hand. "I'm Dagny. But I'm not a fellow. I'm a girl."

"I'm not a fellow either," said Megan. "Once I wrote a rhyme for my Mom. Wanna hear it? *Roses are red, violets are blue, you give me an allowance, so I love you!*"

Mr. Harcourt started to laugh. He laughed so hard he was shaking and he dropped his cane. He was still laughing when Megan handed his cane back to him and they said good-bye.

They stopped next at a house where a boy was washing a white car. His shoes were on the steps of the house and his bare feet were covered in soapy suds. A black puppy ran around in circles

31

barking at Dagny and Megan.

They said "hi" and the boy nodded to them. He looked like he was in about grade three.

He had freckles, and his nose was peeling. Dagny thought he had a nice smile.

"Do you think your Mom might want to order some cherries?" asked Dagny.

The boy shook his head. "I've got my very own cherry tree. My Mom orders cherries from me."

Megan gave Dagny a poke and pointed to the steps. The puppy was dragging away one of the shoes.

The boy looked over. "Hey!" he cried. Then he started to chase the puppy round and round the car.

The puppy ran out onto the lawn, then stopped. He ran back towards the boy, then darted away again.

Dagny and Megan joined in the chase. They ran all around the house and finally cornered the puppy in the garage where Dagny caught him up in her arms. The boy pulled his shoe free.

"Thanks," he said. "I'm Chris."

"I'm Dagny. And that's my almost-best friend, Megan."

Megan nodded. "You can play with us if you want."

"We're visiting at Waxwing," said Dagny, "with my Aunt Allie."

"Is that the lady with one long braid down the middle of her back?" asked Chris.

"Yup," said Dagny. "I've got one long braid down the middle of my back too. See?"

She twisted around to show him.

"Maybe I'll play sometime," said Chris.

"Well, bye!" said Dagny. "We're getting zillions of orders for cherries."

Chris waved and the puppy barked.

Dagny and Megan tried six more houses. But it was no use. Nobody wanted any cherries.

The walk home seemed to take forever. They stopped to get a drink of water from a lady's hose. When they finally turned into the gravel driveway, they saw Aunt Allie waving to them from the porch.

"We tried to get orders for cherries," Dagny told her. "But nobody wanted any."

Aunt Allie smiled. "Everybody in Cherryland has a tree or two of their own."

"Whew!" said Megan, as she plopped down on the porch step. "We walked forever!"

"Why don't you put on your bathing suits?" said Aunt Allie. "After you have a bite to eat, you can cool off under the sprinklers in the orchard."

"Yahoo!"

Dagny and Megan raced upstairs lickety-split.

"We didn't walk forever," said Dagny.

"Well, it was *almost* forever!" said Megan.

"Yes." Dagny nodded. "Almost."

# CHAPTER 6

THEY PLAYED UNDER THE SPRINKLERS UNTIL THEY
were shivering and their lips were blue.

Megan pretended she was a monster and chased
Dagny all around the cherry trees until Dagny suddenly turned and spit.

"Stop it!" gasped Megan. "You almost spit right in
my eye!"

"I was spitting at the monster," said Dagny.

"It's supposed to be *pretend* spit!"

Just then they heard a faint "hallooo!" from behind
the shed, and Aunt Allie came around the corner.

"Aaah! Here you are!" she said. "I have to go into
town to rent a rug shampooer for the day. To spruce
the place up a bit in case I sell it. Anyway, I thought
it might be fun to eat out! We could have an early
supper. Maybe Chinese food."

"With fortune cookies?" asked Megan.

"Of course!" said Aunt Allie. "We'll go as soon as
you change into some dry clothes."

"I never had Chinese food before!" cried

34

Dagny, as she raced away with Megan. "What's a fortune cookie?"

"Well...it's not like a real cookie," said Megan. "It doesn't have any taste."

Dagny scrinched up her face. "You mean like a sugar-free cookie?"

"Only better," said Megan. "When you open it up, there's a piece of paper inside. And it's got your fortune on it."

"What's a fortune?"

"It tells something that's going to happen to you."

"Like what?"

"Like maybe you'll get lots and lots of money!"

Dagny was grinning as they stood dripping puddles onto the bedroom floor. If she got lots and lots of money, then Aunt Allie could hire pickers and she wouldn't have to sell Waxwing!

They were dressed in a flash, Dagny in her purple polka-dotted dress and Megan in a pink skirt and a pink blouse, with a pink ribbon in her hair. Then they sped away in Aunt Allie's canary-yellow sports car, leaving clouds of dust behind them.

They stopped at a store with a sign in the window *Rent a Rug Shampooer For a Day!* After loading the shampooer into the car, they walked across the street to an art-supply store, and Aunt Allie bought three tubes of red paint. Then they went into a restaurant with orange-plastic flowers everywhere. A white-haired man and a lady were sitting at one table. A grandma, a mom, and a red-headed boy about five-years-old were sitting at another table.

Aunt Allie ordered food with funny names.

"Do they have any moo goo french fries?" asked Dagny.

The waitress smiled, then walked away with her heels clicking.

Dagny took lots of the chicken balls, an in-between scoop of rice, and just a pinch of the slippery vegetables. She had to put a hand over her mouth to hold back the laughter when they tried eating with chop sticks.

"I DON'T LIKE THIS FLOOR!"

Dagny turned around. It was the red-headed boy. He was kicking the floor with the toe of his shoe.

Dagny and Megan looked at each other, and then at the floor. It was just plain old blue and white tiles.

"Ouch!" Now the grandma was rubbing her knee. "Stop it, Timbo! Stop kicking Grandma!"

Dagny's eyebrows shot up. She'd never heard of anyone kicking a grandma before! When the boy turned around in his chair, Dagny stuck her tongue out at him.

"THAT GIRL STUCK HER TONGUE OUT AT ME!"

The white-haired couple turned and looked at Dagny. And then the mother of the boy said in a loud voice, "Never mind, Timbo. *Some* people have no manners!"

Dagny scrunched down low in her chair. She kept her head bent and stared at her straggly shoe laces under the table. When she looked up again, Aunt Allie winked at her.

Then the grandma and the mom and Timbo got up and left.

Megan patted Dagny on the shoulder, and whispered in her ear, "You do so have manners!"

"I never kick grandmas," said Dagny. "No matter what!"

"Me neither," said Megan.

Dagny wondered if the waitress would come over and ask her to leave. Maybe she would say Dagny wasn't behaving properly. Dagny chewed her food with her lips held together tightly just in case the white-haired people were watching. They would see that she had very good manners and never chewed with her mouth open.

"Excuse me for bothering you, Aunt Allie," said Dagny, in a voice loud enough to be heard at the next table, "but would you please pass the pepper, if it wouldn't be too much trouble?"

Aunt Allie smiled. "No trouble at all, Dagny."

"Thank you very much," said Dagny. "I never reach across the table."

Megan looked over at the white-haired people and said, "She never puts her elbows on the table either!"

But Dagny *did* have her elbow on the table. She moved it off so fast that she knocked over her glass of milk and it spilled all over her slippery vegetables!

"Oh no!"

"Never mind, Dagny," said Aunt Allie. "I'm sure the waitress will get you another plate. And there's more vegetables in the dish."

Dagny shook her head. "I ruined my share. I shouldn't be allowed anymore. Not even a pinch."

"You're just saying that because you don't like them!" said Megan.

"You don't know what I like, Megan Canary!"

37

"Ha!"

"Ha yourself!"

The waitress brought the fortune cookies and they forgot all about slippery vegetables.

Aunt Allie opened hers first. *"Look no further than your own backyard."*

"See, Aunt Allie?" cried Dagny. "That means you shouldn't sell Waxwing!"

Aunt Allie just smiled a sad smile.

Then Megan read her fortune next. *"There is no greater gift than a friend."*

This time it was Megan who smiled a sad smile.

Dagny took the last fortune cookie from the plate. She was sure it would say something about getting lots and lots of money! The cookie crumbled when she broke it open. She pulled out a white slip of paper and read the words, *"You will succeed if you keep trying."*

Dagny slumped back in her chair. Not a thing about money! And they didn't have very much time to keep trying. The cherries would be ripe soon. She ate a bit of the cookie.

It tasted yucky.

On the drive home, Dagny looked at all the roadside stands along the way.

"There's too many people selling cherries," she said. "They won't make much money."

"Well, Mr. Harcourt does okay at his stand," said Aunt Allie. "But that's because he gives something extra with the cherries."

"What does he give that's extra?" asked Megan.

"Take a look and see," said Aunt Allie as she

slowed down and gave a toot of the horn.

Mr. Harcourt waved his cane to them from behind his freshly painted cherry stand. There was a big sign on top, *Free Glass of Lemonade with Cherries*.

"People like something extra," said Aunt Allie. "And they get thirsty driving along these dusty roads."

Dagny felt the white slip of paper in her pocket, and turned to Megan. "Do the fortunes always come true?"

"Not always," said Megan.

"*Almost* always?"

"Yes." Megan nodded. "Almost."

# CHAPTER 7

WHEN THEY GOT BACK TO WAXWING, DAGNY AND Megan raced upstairs to change.

As Dagny scrambled into shorts and a too-big tee-shirt, Megan looked over at her.

"How come you're grinning like that?" she asked.

Dagny gave her eyebrows a little wiggle up and down. "I know how we can solve the cherry problem!" she said, with another big grin.

"How?"

"We can sell cherries with something extra, that's how!"

"You mean, lemonade?"

Dagny shook her head. "Something way better than that!"

"Cookies?"

"Guess again."

Megan kept guessing for a little while, then she gave up.

"Fortunes, of course!" said Dagny.

Megan giggled. "Fortune cherries?"

41

"Sure!" said Dagny. "We can pick black cherries from the front yard, and put a fortune in every bag! Then we can sell them at our own roadside stand! Aunt Allie can hire pickers with the money we make!"

Megan clapped her hands. "And when the pickers come, we can sell a zillion more fortune cherries!"

They hurried outside and set to work making up fortunes. Megan sat on the pit-spitting tree stump while Dagny perched on the old swing with the cracked seat. They wrote and they wrote. It took them a long time, but they stuck with it. No matter what, they were going to solve the cherry problem.

Dagny thought she caught a glimpse of something moving out of the corner of her eye. She looked towards the orchard, but she didn't see anything. Then it happened again. She turned her head quickly to the left. Something stirred behind the branches of a cherry tree. Then she spotted Chris. He was creeping towards them from tree to tree. Dagny tugged on Megan's tee-shirt and pointed. Megan giggled.

Suddenly Chris burst out from behind a tree and stood on the lawn with his hands on his hips, yelling, "Bet you can't catch me!"

Dagny and Megan gave chase. They ran very fast, laughing and shouting as they zigzagged through the orchard. After a very long time, they collapsed on the grass, puffing.

When Dagny caught her breath, she told Chris about their fortune cherry idea and read one of her fortunes. *"A kitten will follow you home."*

"Do they get to keep it?" asked Megan.

Dagny nodded. "Except if they live in an apartment because then they're not allowed."

Chris blinked. "You can't have a kitten in an apartment?"

As Dagny and Megan were shaking their heads, they heard a hissing sound. The black cat with the white paws was staring down at them from a cherry tree. His back was arched and he looked mad.

"It's not our fault!" Megan shouted up to him. "It's a rule!"

"Well...you can have turtles and fish and birds," said Dagny. "Anna even had a pet snake."

"Dangerous beasts shouldn't be allowed in apartments," said Megan. "They might get loose."

"Anna's snake wasn't a killer snake," said Dagny. "It was just a plain old snake."

"Ha!" said Megan. "Plain old snakes can still give people the willies."

Chris scrunched up his face. "What's the willies?"

"I'm not sure," said Megan. "But snakes always give my Mom the willies, so she won't go near them."

Chris was chewing a big wad of gum. He blew a pink bubble, then sucked it back into his mouth. "I've got a dog and a cherry tree of my own," he said. "And I named them both Barky."

"I wish I could have a cherry tree for a day," said Dagny.

Megan looked at her. "Just for one day?"

Dagny nodded. "A day when the cherries are ripe!"

A shadow fell over them. It was Aunt Allie. She was smiling. She had a towel wrapped

43

around her head and a few strands of wet hair hung down around her neck.

"I'd want the cherries to be ripe too!" she said. And she put a big plate of banana bread on the grass in front of them. "Please help yourselves. This was one of my grandmother's favourite recipes!"

Chris put his gum on his nose, then took a big bite. "It's good!"

Aunt Allie said she was tickled pink to hear it, then went back into the house.

Dagny read another fortune. *"You will get lost in the jungle, but then you will get found again."*

"Who finds them?" asked Megan.

"You don't have to know that," said Dagny.

"Ha!" said Megan. "What if they get found by a giant gorilla with fangs?"

Chris shook his head. "Gorillas don't have fangs."

"So, maybe they get found by a giant spider!" said Megan. "One that puts sticky spit all over them and glues them to its web!"

Dagny scribbled something on her notepad. "There!" she said. "I put they get found by a nice grandma."

"Grandmas don't go into jungles," said Chris.

"Well, this one does!" said Dagny. "That's because she loves jungles more than anything and she's trying to get away from a mean boy named Timbo who kicks her right in the knee all the time, very hard!"

"Oh," said Chris.

"My turn!" said Megan. *"You will win a medal because you will be very brave."*

"What do they do that's brave?" asked Chris.

Megan thought for a moment. "Um...they trip a bank robber and then they sit on him until the police come."

Chris nodded.

"Here's another one," said Megan. *"You will swallow your gum by accident."*

"I never do that," said Dagny. "I always spit it out."

"You're not supposed to," said Megan. "Somebody might get gum on the bottom of their shoe."

"I stick gum on my nose and then I chew it later," said Chris.

They made up fortunes until the evening shadows grew longer and Chris had to leave, then they hunted for a hammer and some nails inside the shed. They found them hidden in a bucket behind a fancy ride-on lawn mower, so they set to work building a roadside stand from old crates. While they worked, Dagny made up a story about the Princess Tickled-Pink.

"Once upon a very long time ago," she said, " there was a Princess Tickled-Pink who giggled all the time, even when her Mom was getting mad at her. So one day, the King said he would give gold coins to anybody who could make the Princess stop giggling."

Megan looked over at Dagny. "Is this going to be the part about the very brave girl?"

"Maybe it is, maybe it isn't," said Dagny.

"I bet it is," said Megan.

"Ha!" said Dagny. "There was a very brave *boy* who wanted the gold coins so his mother would never ever have to go to work anymore. And he spied on the Princess Tickled-Pink. And he saw her eating cherries all the time because she loved them so much. And everytime she popped a cherry into her mouth, she started to giggle. That's how the very brave boy guessed that the cherries had giggle pits."

"How come they had giggle pits?" asked Megan.

"Because a mean wizard planted a cherry tree with giggle pits in the royal garden," said Dagny. "He wanted to get the Princess Tickled-Pink in trouble all the time."

"How come?"

"Because he was mean!"

"Oh."

"So anyway," said Dagny, "after the Princess spit them out, the brave boy put all the giggle pits into a bag and went off to find the mean wizard. He walked forever and ever until he finally found the wizard asleep in a field. That's when he dumped the giggle pits all over the wizard. The giggle pits tickled the wizard's nose and he sneezed a gigantic sneeze. He sneezed so hard that the giggle pits flew all over the Kingdom. And wherever they landed, a cherry tree with giggle pits grew. The end."

"The end?" said Megan. "What about the Princess? Did she still get into trouble for giggling?"

"Nope."

"How come?"

"Because *everybody* had a cherry tree with giggle pits," said Dagny, "so everybody giggled all the time!"

It was starting to get dark so they sat in the light from the opened kitchen door, and made a sign to go on their stand.

*"Fortune Cherries — Almost Always Come True!"*

Just as they were finishing up, Aunt Allie called out in a sing-songy voice that it was time to come in.

Dagny held the screen door open for Megan. "I've got good manners, don't I?"

"Sometimes you spit in people's eyes," said Megan.

"I did not spit in your eye!" said Dagny. "I missed."

"Well, you *almost* spit in my eye," said Megan.

"Yes." Dagny nodded. "Almost."

# CHAPTER 8

THE NEXT MORNING, DAGNY AND MEGAN FILLED TEN lunch bags with black cherries from the front yard, and dropped a fortune into every bag. Then they waited at their roadside stand for cars to stop. They jumped up and down and flapped their arms, but the cars kept going by with clouds of dust billowing up behind. Every now and then, they ran to the house to get a glass of lemonade or a piece of banana bread, and some sandwiches at lunchtime, but they always counted their bags of cherries when they got back to make sure none were missing.

After awhile, they climbed up a tree at the road's edge to keep the dust from getting in their eyes. Dagny let her sandals drop to the ground and swung her bare feet in the air.

"See that cloud?" she said. "It looks just like a princess in a long gown that goes swish."

Megan nodded. "With golden curls like mine."

"Your curls aren't golden," said Dagny. "Your curls are plain yellow."

"My curls are *so* golden!"

"Who cares?" said Dagny. "I've got flowing hair."

"What's that?" asked Megan.

"It's hair that flows down over your shoulders," said Dagny. "Like a princess."

"Ha!" said Megan. "It does not flow. It's tied back in a crooked braid with little bits sticking out all over the place!"

Dagny pulled the elastic band from the one long braid that hung down the middle of her back and shook her hair loose. "There!" she said. "Now it's flowing all over my shoulders and one day it will be long enough to sit on!"

Megan made a face. "Who wants to sit on their hair?"

"Princesses. That's who!"

"Princesses don't have plain brown hair," said Megan. "They have golden curls."

"My hair's not plain brown," said Dagny. "It's brunette."

"I never heard of that."

"That means *fancy* brown hair," said Dagny. "I'm the Princess Dagnatunia with flowing brunette hair!"

"Well, I'm the Princess Meganilla with golden curls!"

Just then they heard a car grinding to a stop.

Dagny clapped her hands. "A customer! Maybe they'll want to buy lots and lots of..."

She stopped in mid-sentence as she peeked down through the branches. There was a dull thud of a car door followed by the crunching of footsteps.

49

"Come on!" said Megan.

But Dagny didn't budge.

Megan looked at her. "Aren't you coming?"

"It's...it's her!"

"Who?"

"Timbo's Mom!"

Megan craned her neck to get a peek. "Oh, yeah."

"She'll say I don't have good manners," whispered Dagny.

"Don't worry," said Megan. "I'll go. I didn't stick my tongue out or anything."

Dagny could see the top of the lady's shoulders and the sunglasses pushed up on her head.

As Megan scrambled down, the mom asked, "How much are your cherries?"

"Just one dollar for the whole bag," said Megan. "And you get a fortune inside. You don't have to pay for that part. It's free."

"Are they nice cherries?"

Megan's head was bobbing up and down. "Very nice and juicy and black! And you can spit the pits really far!"

"It's rude to spit," said the mom.

"I would *never* spit in someone's eye," said Megan.

Dagny's heart started thumping. Maybe Megan would point up to her. Maybe she would tell the mom that there was a girl sitting in the tree who had bad manners and had almost spit right in her eye! Dagny tightened her grip on the branch and hitched herself over so she was hidden by the leaves. The branch creaked and the mom tipped her head back to look up into the tree.

Dagny held her breath and kept very still.

**HONK, HONK. HONK, HONK, HONK.**

The mom turned and walked back to the car. "Stop it, Timbo! Mommy doesn't like you honking the horn."

**HONK, HONK. HONK, HONK, HONK.**

Dagny had an idea. She pulled the notepad and the chewed-up pencil from her back pocket and scribbled a few sentences. She tore out the page, shoved the notepad and pencil into her pocket again, and began to lower herself quietly over the branches. She dropped to the grass and crept low behind the crates. Lifting her head, she peeked over.

The mom turned and started back. Dagny ducked her head just in time. She reached up over the edge of the crate, felt for a bag of cherries and stuffed the paper inside. Then she pushed the bag towards Megan with a "Psst!"

Megan slid a glance in Dagny's direction, picked up the bag and held it out.

"My Timbo likes cherries," said the mom. "I hope they're good."

**HONK, HONK. HONK, HONK, HONK.**

There was another thud of the car door as the mom got back inside.

**I WANT A POPSICLE!**

As the car started up, Dagny lifted her head. Timbo looked out the window at her.

Dagny crossed her eyes and stuck out her tongue. Timbo's mouth dropped open as the car pulled away in a cloud of dust.

"What did you put in the bag?" asked Megan.

Dagny popped up from behind the crates. "Another fortune."

"What did it say?"

*"Never kick a grandma. No matter what!"*

Dagny and Megan grinned at each other. And they were still grinning when they got back from a trip into town with the rug shampooer. They sat in the tree all afternoon waiting for more cars to stop, but it was almost suppertime before a green car pulled over and a lady with puffy hair and sunglasses poked her head out the window.

"Would you like to buy some fortune cherries?" asked Dagny.

Megan held up a bag. "I know where there's a good one about a kitten!"

"Aaah!" said the lady. "I like kittens. Maybe I'll buy a bag."

The lady gave them a dollar. She rolled up her window, then she rolled it down again.

"I wonder if you could help me," she said. "I'm looking for Waxwing Orchards. Do you know if I'm going the right way?"

"It's at the end of this driveway," said Dagny. "My Aunt Allie lives there!"

"Oh, good! I'm Mrs. Sherman, your aunt's real estate agent. She wants me to sell her farm for her." The lady started rolling the window up again. "Good luck with your cherries!"

As the green car pulled away, Dagny slapped her hand to her heart. "This is *hor*-rible!"

"Double-dip horrible!" said Megan. "We only made a couple of dollars, and now it's too late!"

"It is not too late," said Dagny. "We've still got time to think up something."

"Well, it's *almost* too late," said Megan.

"Yes." Dagny nodded. "Almost."

# CHAPTER 9

THAT NIGHT DAGNY READ ANNA'S LETTER AGAIN while Megan was sleeping.

*Dear Dagny*
*I am doing this letter on my Dad's computer. He said I could. You will think I am a good speller. But I'm not. The computer fixes up spelling mistakes. I will tell you what I did today. I watched TV for fifteen minutes. Then my Mom asked me to wash up. I did. It took one minute to be exact. We went shopping. We bought some milk and some eggs. Then we went to the bakery. I took the number and gave it to the lady. We bought cheese buns. I was really hungry. I begged my Mom for a pizza dog. When I got to the car, I gobbled it up. It was very spicy so it burned my mouth of course. Then a total disaster happened. I tried to drink my pop and it leaked all over the car and all over me. So I had to sit in the car when my Mom went into the drugstore to buy toothpaste. A big dog barked at me. I honked the horn at it. The rest is a boring day. I don't*

*have anybody to play with here. Not one person. I bet
you don't either. Do you miss me? I miss you. I wish
I didn't move.*
                    *Your best friend forever and ever,*
                    *Anna*

Anna was still her best friend even if she was
having fun with Megan. Dagny folded the letter
and slipped it under her pillow, her too-fat pillow. She liked her own skinny pillow better.

Suddenly she felt homesick. She missed the
little things. The way her mother hummed
when she was folding the laundry and the way
she tucked Dagny in at night. The way the blue
curtains in her bedroom sagged in the middle
where some hooks were missing at the top. The
way her bare feet prickled on a corner of the liv-
ingroom rug where glue had spilled and hard-
ened.

When Megan mumbled something in her
sleep, Dagny propped herself up on an elbow
and listened to the slow breathing coming from
the next bed. She wished Megan would wake up.
She wanted to jump up and down on her, but
instead she just creaked her way across the
floorboards to the other bed.

"Megan? Are you awake?"

Megan didn't answer.

Dagny put her face very close to Megan's and whispered louder, "Are you awake?"

Still no answer.

She pushed up Megan's eyelids with her fingertips.

"What...?!" Megan jerked away, rubbing her eyes.

"Are you awake?"

"Sort of."

Dagny ran back to her own bed. "I'm awake too."

Megan's voice was sleepy. "I was having a dream."

"What about?"

Megan lifted her arms and stretched. "We were singing on a street corner and people were throwing gold coins to us."

"How come?"

"Because people do that," said Megan. "Once I saw a man singing and playing the guitar on the street and people were throwing money right into his hat!"

Dagny was twisting the fringe on the bedspread. She was busy thinking.

"Know what?" she said. "I just got the greatest idea in the whole world!"

"Hmmm?" Megan had curled up into a ball and was almost asleep again.

"And it's way better than fortune cherries!" said Dagny.

"What is it?"

"Guess."

"Give me a hint."

"It's kinda like your dream."

"I don't get it," said Megan.

"Give up?"

"Yup."

Dagny let out a little squeal. "We can go door-to-door singing for the neighbours and they'll give us lots and lots of money! Then Aunt Allie can hire pickers!"

Megan didn't say anything.

"Are you still awake?"

But the only sound was the chirping of the crickets outside. Sleepy and sunburned and happy, Dagny closed her eyes and dreamed about getting zillions of gold coins and becoming a famous singer on the radio.

The next morning, they darted outside so quickly that Dagny's arms were still covered in soap suds from washing the breakfast dishes.

"Hmmm," she said, looking Megan up and down. "I think people will give us more money if we look poor."

Megan put her hands on her hips. "We *are* poor!"

"We have to look even poorer!"

"How?"

"Easy!" said Dagny. "Do this!"

Dagny yanked out the lining of her empty shorts pocket. Then Megan turned her pockets inside-out too.

"There!" said Dagny. "Now everybody will see we don't have a pinch of money!"

"Maybe we should look sad too!" said Megan.

They made their mouths droop down at the corners, then they looked at each other and started to laugh.

Arm in arm, they set off down the road, enormous buckets slapping against their bare legs. They stopped once to pull a handful of cherries off a low branch, then hurried on their way.

Their first call was at Mrs. Armstrong's. Dagny knocked on the door, then pressed her nose against the screen. She could see a fly buzzing around, trying to get out. After she hollered, "Anybody home?" she heard the flip-flip-flop of sandals in the hall.

"You've got a smudge on your nose," said Megan.

Dagny spit into her palm and rubbed her nose. "Is it gone?"

"Yup."

Mrs. Armstrong half-opened the door. The fly zoomed out.

"Oh, hello girls!"

Dagny and Megan burst into song.

*"We can eat a zillion cherries,*
*We can eat them lickety-split,*
*But even if we're hungry,*
*We'd never eat a pit!"*

They sang it over and over again about ten times.

When they were finished, Mrs. Armstrong just stared at them.

"That's it," said Dagny. "We're done now."

Mrs. Armstrong blinked. "Oh!" she said. "Well, don't go away. I've got something for you!"

The flip-flip-flop of her sandals faded away as she went back along the hall.

"That was a good song to sing!" said Dagny. "It makes us sound very poor."

"I think Mrs. Armstrong's gonna give us lots of money!" whispered Megan.

Mrs. Armstrong came back holding a brown paper bag.

"Here you go!" she said. "It just so happens I made a fresh batch of cookies with tons of chocolate chips!"

Dagny and Megan thanked her, and tried not

to look disappointed.

"We should have told Mrs. Armstrong we were carrying *money* buckets," said Megan, when they were out of earshot.

Dagny opened the bag and pulled out a cookie. "We'd better eat them before the chocolate chips get all melty." And she took a giant bite. Megan reached into the bag too. "Mmmm! I love sugar cookies!"

Just before they got to Mr. Harcourt's roadside stand, they licked the chocolate from their fingers, then they sang their cherry-pit song, holding their buckets in their arms. Megan did a fancy leap and a twirl, finishing with a big "ta-daah!"

Mr. Harcourt gave them each a glass of lemonade. They gulped it down and chewed on the ice cubes.

A bit further down the road, they found Chris sitting under his cherry tree, tossing a baseball from one hand to the other.

*Thunk, thunk. Thunk, thunk, thunk.*

Dagny and Megan slumped down beside him.

"Wanna play?" he asked.

Megan shook her head. "We're going door-to-door singing for money."

"Did you get any?"

"Any what?" asked Megan.

"Money."

"Nope," said Dagny. "Just cookies and lemonade."

Chris peeked into the buckets. "Where are they?"

"Where are what?" asked Dagny.

"The cookies!"

"We ate them," said Megan.

Dagny stretched out on the grass and looked up at

the sky peeking through the leaves.

"Be careful not to look at the sun," said Megan. "You'll go blind if you look at the sun."

"I *never* look at the sun," said Dagny.

"You can go blind if you look at the moon too," said Chris.

Dagny shook her head. "You cannot!"

"I mean, you can go deaf," said Chris.

Dagny crossed her legs and dangled a sandal from her toe. "You cannot go blind *or* deaf if you look at the moon!" she said. "The moon cannot hurt you one little bit!"

"Oh, yeah?" said Chris. "A full moon can make people act crazy!"

Dagny and Megan turned to look at him. He was holding up his arm as a purple-and-white caterpillar crept around his wrist.

"It's true!" he said. "Once my aunt came over for dinner and she wouldn't sit down at the table. She said it was better to eat standing up. And my Dad said, 'Oh, then your food can go straight down to your hollow leg without coming to any bend at your lap, eh?' And my aunt threw a brussel sprout at my Dad and hit him right on the nose!"

Dagny's mouth dropped open. "Did she really throw a brussel sprout?"

Chris nodded. "I saw it with my own eyes. And when she left, my Dad said it must be a full moon. And you know what? It was!"

Dagny rolled onto her stomach. "My Aunt Allie would *never* throw food."

"No matter what!" added Megan.

Chris flicked the caterpillar from his arm and started throwing the ball from one hand to the other again.

*Thunk, thunk. Thunk, thunk, thunk.*

"Are you gonna play baseball?" asked Megan.

Chris shook his head. "Nobody to play with."

"How come?" asked Dagny.

Chris shrugged a little. "No kids my age live around here," he said.

*Thunk, thunk. Thunk, thunk, thunk.*

"Know what?" said Megan. "I don't even have a best friend."

*"Almost!"* said Dagny.

Megan sighed. "That's not the same thing."

"We gotta go," said Dagny. And she jumped to her feet before Megan could say another word about best friends.

They trudged on from house to house, but when they finally headed home, their money-buckets were still empty. Dagny kicked at the stones as they walked along, stirring up little clouds of dust.

"Never even got one cent for all that singing!" she said.

"We got cookies and lemonade and...."

"And not one cent!"

Megan turned and walked backwards in front of Dagny. "It was good singing too!"

"Not good enough to be on the radio," said Dagny.

"Well, it was *almost* good enough."

"Yes." Dagny nodded. "Almost."

# CHAPTER 10

WHEN THEY GOT BACK TO WAXWING, THEY FOUND A *For Sale* sign on the front lawn. They wanted to kick it, the way Timbo had kicked the blue and white tiles. But instead, they ran to find Aunt Allie. She was in the backyard, splashing one of her canvasses with pizzazz.

"This isn't a fun day!" said Dagny.

"Well, I had an idea," said Aunt Allie. "And I think it just might cheer you up."

Dagny wrinkled her forehead. "A way to solve the cherry problem?"

"I'm afraid not," said Aunt Allie. "But I'm pretty sure you'll like it anyway. Remember the other day when we got back from the restaurant and I brought the banana bread out to you?"

Dagny and Megan nodded.

"Well," said Aunt Allie, "I heard you talking about how you'd like to have a cherry tree for one day."

"A day when the cherries are ripe!" said Dagny.

Aunt Allie grinned. "That's right! Anyway,

I've been thinking, why not?"

"Why not what?" asked Dagny.

"Why not have your own tree-for-a-day!" said Aunt Allie.

Dagny gasped. "Really?"

"I'd be tickled pink if you would!" said Aunt Allie. "You can put your names on your own trees, and as soon as the cherries are ripe, you can pick them!"

They thanked Aunt Allie about a zillion times, then they linked arms and went up and down the rows of cherry trees, looking for just the right one. It was hard to choose when they thought there might be a tree just a little better in the next row! But then they saw it at the same time. The perfect tree! It was bigger than all the others and loaded with cherries!

Megan pointed right at it. "I pick that one!"

Dagny sucked in her breath. "I was just going to say that!"

"Too late," said Megan. "I said it first."

"That's not fair!"

"Is too!"

Dagny put her face very close to Megan's. "It's *my* aunt's farm!"

"*Almost* aunt!" said Megan. "*Almost* farm!"

Dagny wanted to bop Megan Canary! She pulled a daisy from the ground and swatted her right on the nose!

"Don't!" squealed Megan. "You can poke somebody's eye out like that!"

"You cannot!" said Dagny. "You cannot poke somebody's eye out with a daisy!"

"Yes, you can! So just stop being such a bully!"

"Stop being such a pig!"

"I am *not* a pig!" shouted Megan.

"Yes, you are!" Dagny shouted back. "And this is *so* a farm because there's a pig here! And that's you! Oink, oink, oink!"

Megan marched away and sat down in the dappled shade of the perfect cherry tree.

Dagny stood swatting at the long grass with a stick. *Swish, swish. Swish, swish, swish.*

She wanted that tree, the perfect tree. But she knew Megan really had said it first.

"Megan?"

Megan didn't answer. Her arms were folded and she looked mad.

"Megan, know what? I had an idea."

Megan still didn't answer. She started humming to herself instead.

"We could share that tree," said Dagny. "There's about a zillion cherries on it."

At first Megan didn't say anything. Then she looked up at the tree.

"My arms *would* get sore," she said slowly, "if I had to pick *all* those cherries."

Dagny gave her a grin. "Deal?"

"Deal!"

They shook on it, then they stood together gazing at the perfect tree.

Dagny tilted her head from one side to the other. "It looks just like the Cherry-Pit Princess."

Megan nodded. "The Cherry-Pit Princess likes herself better as a tree."

They linked arms again as they hurried back to the

picnic table to make name tags to hang on their very own tree-for-a-day.

Dagny painted every letter in her name with a different colour, then she made black and red circles all around the edges of the cardboard. She glanced across the table. Megan was painting little trees on the top of each letter in her name. Dagny wished she'd thought of that.

"What are those black and red circles?" asked Megan.

"Cherries," said Dagny. "Ripe cherries and unripe cherries."

"Oh," said Megan. "I thought they were balloons."

Dagny held her name tag at arm's length and looked at it. The circles really did look like balloons. She painted strings on the balloons, but her brush was too fat. The strings looked fat and ugly.

Aunt Allie came slap-slap-slapping along the stone walkway in her backless sandals. She was carrying a saucer of milk. When she put it on the grass, the black cat with the white paws limped his way out from under the picnic table. He had a stiff leg.

Aunt Allie knelt down and patted his back while he lapped up the milk. "Poor Thing," she said. "You're just a worn-out old cat."

Dagny felt sorry for him. She wished she hadn't called him a dumb cat.

"What's his name?" she asked.

"Poor Thing."

Dagny nodded. "But what's his name?"

Aunt Allie grinned. "That *is* his name. Poor Thing."

"Hmmm," said Dagny. "That's a funny name for a cat!"

Aunt Allie stood up and looked at Dagny's name tag. "What are those black and red circles?"

"Balloons," said Dagny.

"Oh," said Aunt Allie. "I thought they were cherries."

Dagny decided they were cherries after all. Cherries with fat stems. But it needed something. It needed a splattering of pizzazz! She bent the bristles of her brush back with her thumb, then let go. Flecks of red paint splattered all over her name tag. Then she splattered orange and yellow.

"Look!" she said to Megan. But when she held it up, all the splatters of paint dripped down the cardboard. "Oh, no! It's ruined!"

"No, it's not," said Megan. "I can still read your name."

"It looks wonderful with all those colourful drips!" said Aunt Allie. "You have such a great imagination, Dagny!"

"I do?"

"You'd better believe it!" said Aunt Allie. "It's a gift, you know."

"She makes up good stories," said Megan.

Dagny remembered something, and she said in a small voice, "Know what, Aunt Allie? I don't really take piano lessons."

Megan's head jerked up. "You were just kidding, right Dagny?"

"Sort of."

Aunt Allie patted Dagny on the shoulder. "You're

special just the way you are, with or without piano lessons!"

Just then Poor Thing began to lick Dagny's toes, and she laughed and laughed. She was still laughing as she slipped her name tag into a plastic cover, put a bit of string through it, and raced away to hang it very high on the Cherry-Pit Princess tree so it could flap in the breeze.

Grabbing hold of a branch, Dagny braced her feet against the trunk and pulled herself up into the tree. She hung her name tag as high as she could. When she jumped down again, she let out a squeal.

"Ouch, ouch!"

Her braid was standing straight up. It was hooked onto a branch!

Dagny tugged, but her braid stayed where it was. She jumped and twisted, but no matter what she did, the braid wouldn't come loose. She was stuck! What if her braid had to be cut off before she could get free? What if she couldn't have one long braid down the middle of her back anymore? She yelled and yelled until she spotted a flash of yellow hair through the trees.

Megan came to a sudden stop. "How come your hair's like that?" she asked. "How come it's standing straight up?"

"Help me!" cried Dagny. "I'm stuck!"

"Oh. I thought you saw a ghost or something."

Megan grabbed hold of the branch where Dagny's hair was hooked and pulled it down, grunting and straining. When it was low enough, Dagny twisted and tugged until her braid came free.

She reached into her pocket and pulled out a stick of gum. It was her last stick of gum. She gave it to Megan.

"Know what?" said Dagny, looking up at the tree. "The Bing cherries are getting darker."

Megan nodded. "They're ripe and ready for picking."

"No, they're not!" said Dagny.

"Well, they're *almost* ripe."

"Yes." Dagny nodded. "Almost."

# CHAPTER 11

DAGNY AND MEGAN STOOD IN THEIR PYJAMAS looking for something to eat while Aunt Allie was upstairs having a bath.

"I know!" said Dagny. "We can have bread pudding!"

Megan opened the fridge again. "I didn't see any pudding."

"That's because we have to make it," said Dagny, as she took a loaf of bread out of the cupboard. "My grandpa showed me how."

She tore the bread into little pieces and filled two bowls.

"Now what?" asked Megan.

"Milk!" said Dagny, and she drowned the torn-up bread with it.

"Yuck!" cried Megan. "That's not pudding. That's soggy bread!"

"Just wait," said Dagny. "I saved the best part till last." Then she spooned sugar all over the soggy bread. "Ta-daah!"

Megan made a face. "I'm not having any of that!"

Dagny stuck a spoonful of the bread pudding at Megan. "Just try some."

Megan shut her eyes and opened her mouth. She chewed and her eyes popped open.

"It's good!"

"I told you!"

They went out and sat on the back steps in the square of yellow light from the opened kitchen door, eating bread pudding and looking up at the stars. The only sounds were the chirping of the crickets and the splish-splashing of bath water coming from the opened window upstairs.

"I wonder how many stars are up there?" said Dagny.

Megan shrugged. "Sometimes I make wishes on stars."

They were quiet for a minute, then Dagny asked, "Did you make a wish?"

"Yup."

"Me too. What was your wish?"

Megan shook her head. "I can't tell or it won't come true."

"That's only when you blow out the candles on your birthday cake," said Dagny. "It's okay to tell when you wish on a star."

"You tell your wish first," said Megan.

"Okay. I wished we could think up a way for Aunt Allie to keep Waxwing."

"That's a good wish."

Dagny glanced sideways. "What was *your* wish?"

When Megan spoke her voice was quiet, almost a

whisper. "I wished I could be your best friend."

Dagny didn't know what to say, so she didn't say anything. She took a huge spoonful of bread pudding and chewed. They sat in silence for awhile, breathing in the heavy smell of flowers and slapping at the mosquitoes on their bare ankles.

"I can make up a story about how the cherries got called Bing cherries, if you want," said Dagny.

Megan yawned and patted her hand against her mouth. "Okay."

"Once upon a very long time ago," said Dagny, "there was a very bad windstorm. It blew all the cherry trees out of the ground. But a very brave girl said she was going to look for the Princess of the Windstorm. And she wasn't going to stop looking even if it took a hundred years. She said she was going to spit right in her eye for blowing over all the trees! So the brave girl looked and looked. She looked until she was so weak she could hardly pick up a pebble."

"She couldn't even pick up a pebble?" asked Megan.

Dagny shivered and rubbed her arms. "Nope," she said. "But then she found the Princess of the Windstorm and the brave girl said, 'How come you blew over all the cherry trees?' And the Princess said, 'Sorry. I couldn't see where I was going because my hair was in my eyes.' So the brave girl fixed her messy hair. She made one long braid down the middle of her back. Then the Princess was very happy because she could see for the first time. And she made the wind blow backwards all over the world and it blew the trees back into the ground. The end."

"But you didn't say why!"

"Why what?"

"Why they were called Bing cherries!"

"Oh, yeah. I forgot that part," said Dagny. "The brave girl's name was Gertrude Bing-Bing."

"Then why didn't they call them Bing-Bing cherries?" said Megan. "Her name was Gertrude Bing-Bing, wasn't it? Not Gertrude Bing."

"Because."

"Because why?"

"Just because, that's all!"

The screen door squeaked open behind them.

"Aaah, here you are," said Aunt Allie. "It's getting a bit chilly. Why don't you come inside?"

Aunt Allie was wearing a faded blue bathrobe and water was drip-drip-dripping from her one long braid. She put on the kettle while Dagny and Megan sat down at the kitchen table.

"Thanks for letting us have a tree-for-a-day, Aunt Allie," said Dagny.

Megan grinned. "I never thought I'd have my very own tree!"

"I'm tickled pink it makes you happy!" said Aunt Allie.

"Too bad everybody couldn't have a tree of their own for a day," said Dagny. "It sure would be fun if people could rent trees like rug shampooers."

"You'd be rich, Aunt Allie," said Megan, "if you could rent your trees!"

Aunt Allie dropped a tea bag into the pot, then

spun around and clapped her hands.

"What a great idea!"

"It is?" said Dagny.

Aunt Allie's eyes were shining. "Why *can't* people rent cherry trees like rug shampooers? People from the city would probably love to spend an afternoon in the country picking cherries from their very own tree-for-a-day!"

"And you wouldn't need to hire pickers!" said Dagny.

"Why, I think you've come up with the perfect solution to the cherry problem!" cried Aunt Allie, and she threw her arms around them. "And just in the nick of time too! Those cherries are getting riper every day!" They worked together on an ad to put in the city newspaper.

*Rent your own cherry tree-for-a-day.*
*Bing Cherries—black, ripe, and juicy!*
*Pack a picnic lunch and bring the whole family*
*for an afternoon of old-fashioned cherry picking!*
*Phone Waxwing Orchards*
*to reserve your tree right now*
*Only $35.00*

"We're the best thinker-uppers in the whole world!" said Dagny.

Megan looked over at her. "What about scientists?"

"Oh yeah," said Dagny. "Well, we're *almost* the best!"

"Yes." Megan nodded. "Almost."

# CHAPTER 12

As soon as the ad appeared in the city newspaper, the phone began to ring. It rang and rang. Aunt Allie wrote down the names of the people who phoned, then Dagny and Megan ran out to the orchard to tag a tree. It wasn't long before nearly every tree in the orchard had been tagged with somebody's name. There was even a tag with *Mystery Pickers* on it. When they asked who the mystery pickers were, Aunt Allie just smiled a secret smile and said, "You'll just have to wait and see!"

Poor Thing watched from up in the branches while Dagny and Megan decorated their very own tree-for-a-day with ribbons. Megan tied her share with little bows. Dagny let hers hang like streamers so they could blow in the wind. Aunt Allie stood nearby at her easel, working on a secret painting. She said it was her masterpiece, and she wanted it to be a surprise.

Dagny and Megan stood back to get a better look at their tree.

"Now the Cherry-Pit Princess has pizzazz!" said Megan. And she gave a little clap of her hands.

"She already had pizzazz," said Dagny. "She's special just the way she is."

"I know," said Megan. "But now she's got even more pizzazz!"

"Know what?" said Dagny. "We could make dandelion chains and hang them from the branches!"

Megan grinned. "And we could string popcorn too!" They found a patch of lawn where the dandelions were thickest and set to work, not even taking a break when Chris came over.

Dagny asked him if he wanted to help.

"I don't like dandelions," he said.

"Weeds can be pretty," said Megan.

Chris scrunched up his face. "My Dad sprays dandelions with weed killer!"

"How come?" asked Dagny. "They look nice poking up all over Aunt Allie's lawn! It looks like a princess danced over the grass and a dandelion grew wherever she stepped. Now it's the Great Dandelion Lawn!"

"I never heard of that," said Chris. "But I heard of a real king. He lives right here in Cherryland."

"Ha!" said Dagny.

"It's true!" said Chris. "He's called the Manure King. It says so right on his sign. My Dad buys manure from him."

"What's manure?" asked Megan.

Dagny leaned over and whispered in her ear. "It's animals going to the bathroom."

Megan's eyes widened. "There's a king of *that?*"

Chris did a somersaut on the lawn. "Yup."

Dagny stretched out on the grass beside the chain to measure how long it was. The chain went from the tip of her toes all the way to her neck.

"It needs to be a whole lot longer!" she said.

Megan nodded. "As long as forever!"

After awhile, Chris got tired of watching and went home. But Dagny and Megan kept working until the chain was as long as both of them together, then they hung it from the branches of their tree. After supper, Aunt Allie made them a big bowl of popcorn and they sat on the back steps stringing popcorn with needles and thread.

"I wish we had something special to wear," said Dagny. "For the big cherry-picking day, I mean."

Megan nodded. "I wish we had long gowns that go swish."

The screen door squeaked open. Aunt Allie came out and dumped more popcorn into the bowl. "I think I might have just what you're looking for!" she said.

They followed her upstairs to the attic where boxes and trunks and cobwebs and dust were everywhere.

Aunt Allie fanned her face with her hand. "Whew! It's like an oven up here!" She opened a big black trunk that was covered with stickers from different cities. "Most of this stuff belonged to my grandmother. It's awfully wrinkled, and it simply reeks of mothballs, but you might find something you like!"

"Thanks!" said Dagny.

Aunt Allie stopped on her way to the stairs to look

through a box of books. "Wow!" she cried. "There's a gold mine of information here about growing cherries!" And she left with a pile of dusty old books in her arms.

Dagny and Megan were already busy sorting through the clothes. Dagny chose a long gown with shiny red sparkles all over it, and a hat with an orange feather that was a bit bent. Megan picked out a flowery yellow dress with puffy sleeves and a little black hat with a veil that pulled down over her face.

Dagny wished she had a hat with a veil. "Want to trade?" she asked. "My hat has a really nice feather!"

Megan looked out at Dagny through the black veil. "Nope. This hat looks good with golden curls!"

"So what?" said Dagny. "My dress has sparkles!"

Megan wrinkled up her nose. "I like puffy sleeves better," she said as she pulled a beaded green necklace over her head.

But just then the necklace broke and green beads went flying all over the dusty floorboards!

*Plink, plink. Plink, plink, plink.*

Dagny scrambled to help Megan pick them up, stuffing the runaway beads into the pocket of her sparkly dress.

"What's Aunt Allie going to say?" cried Megan, with a wiggle in her voice.

Dagny patted her on the shoulder. "Don't worry. It was an accident. Anyway, we can fix it. We can string the beads together again, just like popcorn!"

It took them a long time, but they managed to fix the necklace so that it was as good as new. Or *almost* as good as new. After they put it back in the trunk,

79

Dagny felt one more bead in her pocket. She opened her mouth to say something, then closed it again. The necklace looked okay without it.

When they went downstairs, they found Aunt Allie painting at her easel in the kitchen.

"Can we see what you're painting yet?" asked Dagny.

"Soon," said Aunt Allie. "I'm just putting the finishing touches on it."

"Is it another city?" asked Megan.

"Nope," said Aunt Allie. "This time it's something quite different."

When Dagny and Megan were pouring pink lemonade into glasses, Aunt Allie suddenly slapped her forehead with the palm of her hand.

"I just thought of something!" she said. "We should have tagged the trees in alphabetical order. It's going to take ages for people to find their tree."

"We can help them," said Megan.

Aunt Allie smiled. "That would be great!"

"Know what?" said Dagny. "It'd be fun if we had a pit-spitting contest for all the little kids!"

"Good idea!" said Aunt Allie. "We could give the winner some chocolate-covered cherries!"

"Do we have any?" asked Megan.

"No," said Aunt Allie. "But I have some chocolate bars. We can melt them and make our own!"

So they set to work. Megan got a bag of black cherries from the pantry while Dagny unwrapped the chocolate bars and dropped them into a pot on the stove. When the chocolate was nice and melty, Aunt Allie showed them how to hold the cherries by the stems and dip them into the chocolate.

"Oh, I hope you won't have to sell Waxwing, Aunt Allie!" said Dagny, as she licked some chocolate from the back of her hand.

"I'm keeping my fingers crossed," said Aunt Allie. "But it will depend on how many people show up to pick their cherries."

"Don't worry," said Dagny. "I made a wish on a star!"

"I made a wish too," said Megan. "Remember? I wished I could be your best friend. Wishes on stars don't always come true."

"Well..." Dagny tried to think of what to say. "They *almost* always come true."

"Yes." Megan nodded. "Almost."

# CHAPTER 13

THEY CAME IN STATION WAGONS AND JEEPS AND sports cars. They came in pickup trucks and vans and motorhomes. They came with ladders and pails and cameras. They came with lawn chairs and blankets and picnic baskets. And they came looking here, there and everywhere for their very own tree-for-a-day!

While Aunt Allie was shaking hands and collecting the money, Dagny and Megan swished their way up and down the orchard in their long dresses trying to match the families with their trees. Sometimes they found the right tree very quickly, sometimes it took forever. But nobody seemed to mind one little bit. The cherries were black, the sun was shining, and everybody was singing and humming and whistling!

"This is *un*-believable!" said Dagny, her eyes bulging. "There's zillions and zillions of people here!"

"Aunt Allie will be rich!" cried Megan. And her flowery yellow dress swirled as she spun all around.

A frisbee went zooming by. Dagny ran to catch it, but she tripped on the hem of her long sparkly dress, landing with a thud. When she lifted her head, she could see the black cat with the white paws chasing Barky all around the trees.

Chris took a flying leap right over Dagny. He grabbed up the frisbee and sent it whipping through the air just as Dagny was scrambling to her feet.

"Wow!" he said. "There's kids everywhere!"

"This was all our idea, you know!" said Dagny. The hat with the orange feather was tipping down over her eyes. She pushed it back on her head.

Megan gave Chris a little curtsy. "Don't we look nice?" she said, peeking out at him through her black veil.

Chris lifted a shoulder in a shrug. He was busy watching the boys who were wrestling around in the long grass.

"Can't you see?" cried Megan, fluffing up her golden curls. "We look just like princesses!"

Chris suddenly flashed them a big smile. There was something different about him. His front tooth was missing. He poked the tip of his tongue into the gap to show them. Then he ran off to catch the frisbee that came soaring back over their heads.

"Know what?" said Dagny. "We're lucky."

Megan looked at her. "How come?"

"Because we live right across the hall from each other," said Dagny. "Chris doesn't have *any* kids his age around here."

Just then they spotted Mrs. Armstrong coming across the Great Dandelion Lawn. She was carrying her pink and white case with the samples of Sweetheart Beauty Products.

"Hello there!" she called out to them.

Dagny lifted her arms and did a little turn so that Mrs. Armstrong could get a good look at her long, sparkly dress.

"My goodness!" said Mrs. Armstrong. "Don't you girls look lovely!"

"And we hardly even reek of mothballs anymore!" said Dagny.

But Mrs. Armstrong wasn't listening. She was looking around at all the pickers in the orchard. Most of them were knee-deep in the long grass picking cherries from the lower branches, but some were on ladders, and others had climbed right up into the trees to reach the cherries at the very top.

With a little wave of her hand, Mrs. Armstrong headed down a row of cherry trees, calling back to them over her shoulder, "I mustn't dilly-dally!"

Dagny and Megan decided not to dilly-dally either. They got back to work hunting down trees and matching them up with the families. And all the while, people kept arriving in a steady stream, parking on both sides of Aunt Allie's driveway, and in the long grass, and finally on both sides of the dusty road.

Mr. Harcourt arrived too with an old-fashioned ice cream maker and started singing in a wobbly voice, "I scream! You scream! We all scream for ice cream!" Before long, there was a whole line of kids waiting for a chance to turn the handle of the ice cream maker round and round.

It wasn't until blankets were spread out on the long

grass and picnic baskets opened, that Dagny and Megan decided to take a break. They ran back to the house and found Aunt Allie in the kitchen making sandwiches.

"Do you fancy ham or egg salad?" she asked. "I made both, so take your pick!"

They couldn't make up their minds, so they took one of each. Dagny had just taken a big bite when Aunt Allie snapped her fingers.

"Oh, I want to show you something!" she said. Then she went over to her easel, and with a big "ta-daah!" flung back the white cloth hiding her masterpiece.

It was a painting of Dagny and Megan!

For a long moment they just stared at it with their eyes wide and their mouths open.

The masterpiece showed the two of them decorating their Cherry-Pit Princess tree! And Poor Thing was in the painting too, looking down at them from up in the branches.

Dagny slapped a hand to her heart. "It's us!"

Aunt Allie nodded. "What do you think?"

"I think it has pizzazz!" said Dagny, and her eyes were all sparkly. "Double-dip pizzazz!"

"Me too!" said Megan, bobbing her head up and down. "I was just going to say that!"

Aunt Allie grinned. "Thanks. I think it's really the best thing I've ever done. I might even enter it in the Cherryland art show!"

*Tap, tap. Tap, tap, tap.*

A man with a beard was peering at them through the screen door. He was holding a fancy camera. When Aunt Allie went out to talk to him, Dagny and Megan ate their sandwiches lickety-split, then they raced outside to get some home-made ice cream for dessert. Mr. Harcourt only had one flavour. It was black-cherry. But he gave them each a double scoop.

They found a spot in the shade and plopped themselves down cross-legged on the grass, licking at their drippy cones. A teenage girl in a bikini was stretched out on a lawn chair nearby. Mrs. Armstrong was showing her samples of lipsticks.

Megan looked at Dagny. "You've got ice cream on your nose," she said.

"Oops!" Dagny rubbed her nose with the palm of her hand. "Is it gone?"

"Nope."

Dagny was still rubbing it when a girl with braces came running up to them. "Where's the hot dog stand?" the girl asked.

Dagny blinked. "We don't have a hot dog stand."

"How come?"

Dagny shrugged.

"Well," said the girl, "do you sell tee-shirts?"

Dagny shook her head.

The girl threw up her hands. "What kind of place is this?" And she stomped away.

Dagny and Megan looked at each other, then they gave a little shrug and went back to licking their ice cream cones. When they were done, Dagny wiped her sticky hands on the grass. Megan almost wiped her hands too, but she remembered about the spider spit and stopped herself just in time. Then they leaped up and went over to see Aunt Allie. She was standing in the middle of the Great Dandelion Lawn.

The man with the beard was taking her picture.

"This is Tom Drake," she told them. "He's a reporter for the Cherryland newspaper, and guess what? He wants to do a story about our cherry solution!" She put her arms around Dagny and Megan. "It was all their idea, Tom! Don't they make a great team?"

*Click, click. Click, click, click.*

The man with the beard took lots and lots of pictures. When he was finished, Dagny and Megan jumped up and down, hugging each other.

"We're going to be famous!" cried Dagny.

Megan pressed her hands against her cheeks. "Everybody in the whole world will want our autographs!"

A lady with puffy hair and sunglasses came walking by. She turned and looked at Dagny and Megan. "Oh, hi!" she said. "Remember me?"

It was Mrs. Sherman. The lady in the green car who had stopped to buy cherries.

Dagny could hardly believe her eyes! She was holding a kitten!

"This is Pipkin," said Mrs. Sherman, kissing the gray kitten on the nose. "I went to the pound and adopted him. Isn't he a darling?" Then she wiggled Pipkin's paw bye-bye, and walked away.

"I can't believe it!" said Dagny. "The fortune came true!"

"No, it didn't," said Megan. "A kitten was supposed to follow her home. She cheated!"

"Well, it *almost* came true!"

"Yes." Megan nodded. "Almost."

# CHAPTER 14

DAGNY AND MEGAN WENT ALL OVER THE ORCHARD rounding up little kids for the cherry pit-spitting contest, then everybody stood in line by the swing and waited for their turn to sit on the pit-spitting tree stump and spit as hard as they could. There was a boy in green-striped shorts who was bigger than all the others. He looked like he was in about grade five, and he had red hair like Timbo's. Dagny and Megan didn't think it was fair for him to be in the contest, but he looked a bit mean, so they didn't say anything. He kept spitting pits at the little kids.

One by one, everybody had a turn sitting on the tree stump and spitting. When it was the big boy's turn, he sat there spitting twice as far as everybody else. Nobody had a chance.

Dagny handed him the chocolate-covered cherries in a box with a red ribbon. The boy threw the ribbon on the grass and yanked the box open.

Dagny picked the ribbon up. "You're not allowed to litter."

"Says who?"

"Says my aunt!"

The boy started to walk away. Then he stopped and yelled over his shoulder, "That's a dumb hat!"

Dagny didn't say a word. She just stood where she was with tears in her eyes.

"It is *not* a dumb hat!" Megan hollered at him. "It's a very nice hat with an orange feather!"

But Dagny wasn't so sure. Maybe the feather was too bendy. She tried to straighten it, but the feather kept wanting to bend no matter what she did. She sat down on the cracked seat of the old swing and told some of the little kids a story about the monster of the cherry orchard.

"Once upon a very long time ago," she said, "there were two twin princesses of the cherry orchard, Princess Dagnatunia and Princess Meganilla. They were very happy until a monster came along and started eating up all the trees. Princess Dagnatunia said, "Go away! We don't want you here!" And the monster said, "If you can beat me in a pit-spitting contest, I will go away and never come back!" So the Princess Dagnatunia said okay. The monster did a hard spit and the pit went very far. Then the Princess Dagnatunia had a turn and her pit went about as far as forever! The monster said, "How did you do that?" And the Princess said, "Ha, ha! I'm a friend of the windstorm and the wind blew my pit far away!" So the monster left the orchard and he never came back. The end."

The little kids clapped and Dagny bowed.

Just then, Megan came running up, puffing. "You've gotta come see!" she cried, pulling Dagny by the wrist. "It's *hor*-rible!"

Megan led the way, and they went racing through the orchard with their long swishy dresses yanked high above their knees.

"I was gonna put the red ribbon on our tree!" Megan yelled over her shoulder. "The one from the box of chocolates. And that's when I saw him!"

They didn't stop running until they got to their Cherry-Pit Princess tree. The boy in the green-striped shorts was picking cherries from their very own tree-for-a-day. And he was throwing them at Poor Thing! The black and white cat was hissing.

Megan shook her finger. "Stop bothering Poor Thing!" she said. "And you're not allowed to pick cherries from our tree!"

The boy threw another cherry. It landed on Megan's black hat.

Dagny shouted at the top of her lungs. "YOU LEAVE MY BEST FRIEND ALONE!"

Megan's eyes widened. "Am I your *best* friend?"

But Dagny wasn't listening. She was watching the boy picking more cherries.

"That's a killer cat," said Dagny. "He attacks anybody who goes near our tree! He digs his claws right into you and you can't get away, no matter what!"

Just then Poor Thing stretched out on the grass and yawned. Then he blinked and closed his eyes.

The boy laughed. "You call that a killer cat?!"

Dagny felt the bead in her pocket. "You'll be sorry if you eat those cherries."

"Says who?"

"Says me!" answered Dagny. "A scientist used to live here and he..."

Megan looked at her in surprise. "Really?"

Dagny put a finger to her lips to shush her. "....and he did an experiment but it got all scrambled up!"

"Like your brains!" the boy said. And he made a snorting noise.

"Ha!" said Dagny. "The scientist made a mistake and all the cherries on that tree have spinach pits! We put up ribbons to warn people to keep away!"

The boy hooted.

"Just watch!" said Dagny.

She pulled a cherry from the tree, popped it into her mouth and made a face. Then she doubled over, clutching her stomach and groaning. She pretended to spit out the pit. But when she showed it to the boy, it wasn't the cherry pit she was holding. It was the green bead from the broken necklace!

"See?" she said. "A spinach pit!"

Megan let out a giggle, then quickly put a hand over her mouth.

The boy backed up a little. "I hate spinach." He tossed the cherries on the ground and walked away.

"That boy has a cherry-pit heart," said Megan.

Dagny shook her head. "He's got a spinach-pit heart."

"Yeah, a spinach-pit heart," said Megan. Then she grinned. "You made up a good story."

Dagny grinned too. "I know," she said. "It's a gift."

Then Megan tapped Dagny on the shoulder and pointed. There was a boy climbing down from their tree!

He was about five years old. He had red hair.

Dagny and Megan both sucked in their breath at the same time.

It was Timbo! And he was wearing one of their popcorn strings around his neck!

"What's he doing?" whispered Megan.

Timbo was making growling noises as he crouched down and started moving slowly through the long grass.

"Uh-oh!" said Dagny. She pointed to where the Grandma was sitting on a blanket, sprinkling salt onto a boiled egg.

Timbo was creeping closer and closer and closer. When he had sneaked right up behind her, he put a piece of popcorn on the very top of the Grandma's bluey-white hair! And as if that wasn't enough, he kept pulling more and more and more popcorn off the string and adding them to the pile until the Grandma was one big popcorn-head!

It was then that the boy in the green-striped shorts jumped out from behind a cherry tree. Dagny and Megan could hardly believe what happened next! He was holding a water pistol and he squirted it at Timbo, but the water hit the

Grandma smack on the nose! She jumped and popcorn tumbled down all around her.

"Stop it, Jimbo!" she sputtered, holding her hands up in front of her face. "Stop squirting water at Grandma!"

Dagny slapped a hand against her cheek. "Oh, no!" she said in a whisper. "Don't tell me that's Timbo's big brother!"

"Yup." Megan was nodding her head. "Timbo *and* Jimbo! The poor Grandma!"

"I bet it's gonna be a full moon tonight," said Dagny.

"How come?"

"Don't you remember what Chris said?"

"What?"

"His Dad got hit in the nose with a brussel sprout," said Dagny, "and it was a full moon!"

"Oh yeah," said Megan. "And the Grandma got hit in the nose with water!"

**"I WANT TO PUT POPCORN ON YOUR HEAD!"**

Now Timbo was yelling his head off, and stomping all over the long grass. The poor Grandma was just sitting there, dabbing at her wet nose with a napkin and pulling popcorn out of her hair.

"It's disgusting!" said Megan, with her hands on her hips. "And she was minding her own business too!"

"If I were that Grandma," said Dagny, "I'd make a run for it and never come back!"

"Never?" Megan lifted her eyebrows up high. "What about for Christmas?"

"Well," said Dagny. "*Almost* never."
"Yes." Megan nodded. "Almost."

# CHAPTER 15

DAGNY AND MEGAN MADE A SIGN TO KEEP TREE-pirates away from the Cherry-Pit Princess.

*Beware of spinach-pit cherry tree.*
*Very Yucky Cherries!*
*P.S. Watch out for killer cat!!!*

They hung it by a string from one of the lower branches, then they hid out of sight to see if anybody went near their tree. But nobody did, so they went off to play baseball with Chris and the other kids on the Great Dandelion Lawn.

All kinds of families gathered round to watch and cheer them on. And the man with the beard was there too. He took a picture of Megan catching a pop fly in the skirt of her flowery yellow dress. And another one of Dagny sliding home, with her hat down over her eyes and her sparkly red dress twisted every which way.

Around suppertime, blankets were gathered up, toys packed away, and step-ladders folded, as families started to leave. Dagny and Megan kept going back and forth, helping people carry buckets of cherries out to their cars. Everybody tooted their horns good-bye, and sometimes they leaned out their car windows, yelling, "See you next year!"

As the sun was going down and the last few stragglers finally left, Dagny and Megan went inside to have their baths. They were so weary and drooping, they could hardly climb the stairs. But soon, Dagny forgot all about being tired when she looked out the window and spotted Aunt Allie walking in the moonlight. She raced outside in her candy-striped pyjamas with the too-short arms, streaked across the Great Dandelion Lawn and whipped along a row of cherry trees.

"Did you count it yet, Aunt Allie?" she shouted. "Did you get enough money?"

Aunt Allie turned and shouted back, "I'm *afraid* to count it!"

"How come?" Dagny was puffing when she finally caught up to her.

Aunt Allie gave a little shrug. "Just in case."

"In case what?"

"In case I didn't make enough money to keep Waxwing," said Aunt Allie. She was snuggling the black cat with the white paws in her arms, and she sighed a big sigh. "I know growing cherries takes a lot of work, and I have oodles to learn, but I really want to stay and give it a try. I never thought I'd like anything as much as I like painting, but I was wrong."

"But which do you like the best?" asked Dagny, as

they started walking back through the orchard. "Growing cherries or painting?"

"Hmmm," said Aunt Allie. She thought for a moment, then she smiled. "They're both the best!"

After Aunt Allie went into the house, Dagny sat down on the back steps and listened to the leaves stirring in the wind.

*Swish, swish. Swish, swish, swish.*

She thought about Anna kicking a soccer ball farther than anybody, and Megan doing a fancy twirl with an arm curved above her head. She was still thinking when the screen door squeaked open behind her.

"Mom!" Dagny leaped up and threw her arms around her mother.

Mrs. Comfort gave her a big hug. "We wanted to surprise you!"

"We?"

"Mrs. Canary came too!" said Mrs. Comfort. "We decided to spend the week-end picking cherries from our very own tree-for-a-day!"

"But we didn't tag a tree for you!"

"Are you sure?"

A grin crept slowly across Dagny's face. "The mystery pickers!"

"That's us!" laughed Mrs. Comfort. "We were afraid you and Megan would figure it out."

Dagny shook her head. "We thought the Manure King was coming."

Mrs. Comfort's eyes bulged out a little bit, but she didn't say anything. She just sat down on the steps with Dagny. They wrapped their arms around each other, and talked about all sorts of things for a very long time. They talked until Megan and Mrs. Canary peered out at them through the screen door.

"There's a nice pot of tea ready!" said Mrs. Canary.

"Thanks!" said Mrs. Comfort. "I could use a cup." She gave Dagny a little kiss on the top of her head, then got up and went inside.

A moment later, Megan came out, all squeaky clean from her bubble bath. She sat down next to Dagny, spraying drops of water from her wet hair.

"Dagny?"

"Hmmm?"

"Did you mean it?"

"Mean what?"

"Am I really your best friend?"

Dagny nodded slowly. "Yup."

"But what about Anna? Isn't she your best friend anymore?"

"You're *both* the best!" said Dagny.

"Really?"

"You're my best friend that's new and Anna's my best friend that I never see and Chris is my best friend that's a boy!"

Megan thought about this for a moment, then she said, "Well, you're my best friend that's a girl and Chris is my best friend that's a boy. And I can save the last one in case I need it sometime!"

Just then Aunt Allie came around the corner of the house. She was carrying something, but it was too dark to see what it was.

"Did you finish counting the money, Aunt Allie?"

Dagny called out.

"I sure did!"

When she got closer, Dagny and Megan both sucked in their breath. She was carrying the *For Sale* sign from the front lawn!

"I'm just tinkled pink!" she said. "We made over seven thousand dollars today, and there's still more people coming tomorrow!" She tossed the *For Sale* sign face down on the grass. "I won't be needing this anymore!"

"Yippeeeeeee!"

They let out a cheer, then Megan jumped down from the steps. Dagny watched as she leaped and twirled over the grass with her arms and legs flying. Maybe Anna had been wrong about leaping and twirling being silly. Megan didn't look silly. She just looked like she was having fun!

Dagny jumped down and began to leap and twirl too, her one long braid leaping and twirling behind her!

"We're the best dancers in the whole world!" cried Megan.

"Not in the whole world!" said Dagny, laughing. "Just in all of Cherryland!"

"Well, that's *almost* the whole world!" said Megan.

"Yes." Dagny nodded. "Almost."

Then together they shouted out *"ALMOST!"* one more time. And they shouted it right up to the stars!

# ABOUT THE AUTHOR

LYNN MANUEL began her writing career when she moved to British Columbia in the late 1970's. Trained as a teacher, she now loves to share her enthusiasm and knowledge with young people through her mysteries and other stories. She published a mystery series in the 1980's, then branched out to doing books for younger people, including *The Princess Who Laughed in Colours* and *The Night The Moon Blew Kisses*, which was widely reviewed across Canada and the US.

Lynn has her MFA in creative writing from the University of British Columbia. She currently lives in White Rock, BC.